I think we've done it all.
We've played every sport ever invented,

painted more pictures in a day
than van Gogh did in a lifetime,

baked enough biscuits
to feed a small country,

played every board game we could find,

read every comic book th—

OK, OK. Let's stop talking for ten seconds.

All right. Ten seconds of nothing.

I know...

Let's Do Nothing!

Tony Fucile

WALKER BOOKS
AND SUBSIDIARIES

LONDON • BOSTON • SYDNEY • AUCKLAND

We'll pretend we're two statues like you see in the park. You know, carved out of stone and stuff.

Frankie, what are you doing?

SHOOING PIGEONS!!

Shooing pigeons is NOT doing nothing. Let's try again. Let's imagine we're in the middle of a quiet old forest. We're two giant oak trees. You can do that.

I can do that.

That dog over there?
Sleeping on my bed?

What about the Empire State Building in New York? Imagine you're it! Tall. Heavy. You've been sitting still for years and years. No silly pigeon or peeing dog could disturb the likes of YOU! Can you do that?

YEAH!

OK, OK. New plan. I'm going to make you the King of Doing Nothing. Lie down on the floor, please, Sam.

Like this?

YES. Now don't move. And hold your breath, 'cos your tummy's moving up and down.

**OK.
But what if I need to blink...**

THAT'S IT!!

YOU KNOW WHAT...

PEOPLE HAVE GOT IT WRONG FOR

HUNDREDS AND THOUSANDS OF YEARS!

THERE'S **NO WAY** TO DO NOTHING!

YOU, ME, YOUR EYES...

WE CAN NEVER EVER DO NOTHING!

Awwwww...

This is AMAZING.

This is really AMAZING.

You know what we have to do now, don't you?

Yes.

LET'S
DO
SOMETHING!

To Sal and Frankie (the originals),
Stacey, Eli and Elinor

First published 2009 by Walker Books Ltd
87 Vauxhall Walk, London SE11 5HJ

2 4 6 8 10 9 7 5 3 1

© 2009 Tony Fucile

The right of Tony Fucile to be identified as author/illustrator of this work has been asserted by him
in accordance with the Copyright, Designs and Patents Act 1988

This book has been typeset in Myriad Tilt.

Printed in China.

British Library Cataloguing in Publication Data:
a catalogue record for this book is available from the British Library

ISBN 978-1-4063-2135-7

www.walker.co.uk